SPOOKY
and the Wizard's Bats

By Natalie Savage Carlson

Illustrated by Andrew Glass

Lothrop, Lee & Shepard Books
New York

FOR MELISSA,
the granddaughter of our
McCrevan friends
—N. S. C.

FOR SARA AND SARAH
—A. G.

1 2 3 4 5 6 7 8 9 10

Library of Congress Cataloging in Publication Data   Carlson, Natalie Savage.
Spooky and the wizard's bats.
Summary: Spooky, formerly a witch's cat, is plagued by bats sent by a wizard and
thinks of a plan to outwit him.
[1. Cats—Fiction. 2. Magician—Fiction. I. Glass, Andrew, ill. II. Title.
PZ7.C2167Sow 1986   [E]   85-18020
ISBN 0-688-06280-6
ISBN 0-688-06281-4 (lib. bdg.)

The Bascombs had a black cat named Spooky and a white cat named Snowball. Spooky had once belonged to a witch, but he had escaped. Later he rescued Snowball from the very same witch.

Now Spooky and Snowball were both house cats.

At night Spooky liked to go out through the little door cut in the big door. Then he would go pussyfoot, pussyfoot to the bed of begonias. He liked to lie among the begonias and wait for excitement. Sometimes his friend Snowball came too.

One night Spooky went out of the little door in the big door. He went pussyfoot, pussyfoot to the bed of begonias. He lay down among the begonias to listen to the sounds of the night.

"Eek! Eek!" A flight of bats flew in from the hills near the woods. They circled over Spooky. They dove at him. They flew loop-the-loops and barrel rolls and sideslips over the cat. They squeaked shrilly into his ears, *"Eek! Screek!"*

One nipped Spooky's tail.

Spooky knew they belonged to the wizard who
lived in a cave among the hills. He knew this because
when he had belonged to the witch, she would take
him along to visit her brother the wizard.

"Pfft, pfft!" Spooky spat at them as he angrily
clawed the air.

Then he raced quickety-paw to the little door in the big door. He jumped up into the fat chair with the bump in the seat. He spat and clawed at the bats who weren't there.

Later that night the Bascomb family came home from a movie.

"I've never seen so many bats around," said the Bascomb boy. "And they keep circling over our house," said the Bascomb girl.

The next night the bats came again when Spooky was lying among the begonias. He had to race quickety-paw into the house to get away. Now Spooky really was angry!

The very next evening Spooky set out for the wizard's cave in the hills. He wanted to find out just what the wizard was up to. Spooky went pussyfoot, pussyfoot along the street and down a winding road to the hills. Vines hung over the mouth of the cave to hide it. But Spooky knew it was there.

He crept through the vines. He went creepy-crawl, creepy-crawl through the cave. Long stalactites hung from the ceiling. Tall stalagmites pushed up from the floor. A dim light in the distance cast shadows into goblin shapes that pranced around the cat.

At last Spooky reached a rock-walled chamber.
The wizard was seated at a table, poring over a book of
spells and charms. A vase of poison ivy and deadly
nightshade stood at one corner of the table and a
sputtering candle at the other. A wand lay beside the
book. Overhead the bats hung from the stalactites like
brown tassels.

Spooky hid behind a stalagmite. He saw the wizard close the book. He saw the wizard take up the wand and wave it at the bats. He heard the wizard order them, "Begone! Torment that cat!"

The bats let go of the stalactites and took to their wings. They flew out in a dark cloud.

At that moment a great rush of air that smelled like sulfur blew into the chamber. The witch had arrived on her broom. She parked it against the wall.

"So you're sending your bats against that cat as I asked," she cackled. "I hope they drive him back to me, mewling. I want to hear him cry."

"It's the work of my magic wand," the wizard said. "I couldn't make them obey my orders without it."

The witch suddenly wiggled her sharp nose. "I smell *cat!*" she cried.

Spooky scooted away. He raced quickety-paw, quickety-paw between the stalagmites and out of the cave. Halfway home he met the returning bats. They swooped down at him. They squeaked in his ears, "*Eek, screek!*" They nipped at him. Their attack made his paws go faster and faster, quick, quick, quickety-paw.

At last he ran safely through the little door in the big door. He had had enough excitement for one night.

Early the next morning Spooky set out for the cave again. The wizard would be asleep. Spooky had a plan to outwit him.

He pushed through the vines. He went creepy-crawl, creepy-crawl between the stalagmites again. The bats were hanging on the stalactites like tassels. The wizard was snoring on a couch under a cover of rat fur.

Spooky jumped up on the wizard's table.

He picked up the wand between his teeth.

But when he jumped down, he knocked over the vase of poison ivy and deadly nightshade.

The wizard awoke with a snort.

He jumped from his couch and ran after Spooky.

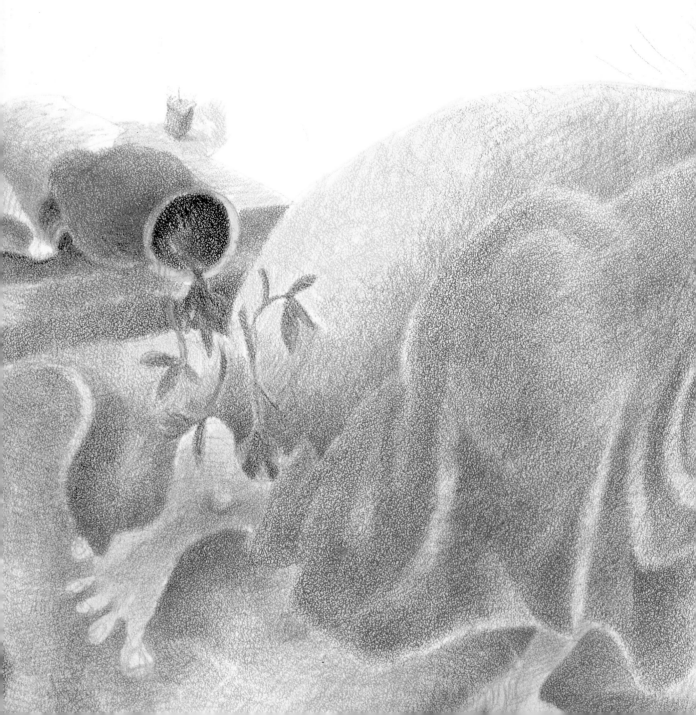

But Spooky beat him to the hanging vines.

Outside a bad storm had suddenly come up. Perhaps the witch had stirred it up to make Spooky drop the magic wand. Wind-driven rain lashed him.

Thunder roared at him. Lightning shot jagged arrows at him. But he dodged them as only a cat can dodge, quick, quick, quickety-paw. He never dropped the wand.

At last Spooky reached home. He went into the living room and dropped the wand among the logs for the fireplace. He shook himself three times to dry off. He jumped into the fat chair with the bump in the seat. Snowball was already there, napping.

Soon the Bascomb family came into the room.
"It's so damp and chilly with all that rain outside,"
said the Bascomb father. "I'll start a fire in the fireplace."

He laid crumpled papers on the andirons. He laid some logs on top of them. He picked up the wand.

"An odd piece of kindling," he said. "I wonder how it got here." He dropped it on top of the logs.

The Bascomb father lit the papers. Soon flames were curling up between the logs.

They reached the wand. The flames turned many colors as they danced over the wizard's wand.

Smoke flew up the chimney like a cloud of ghostly bats. There was roaring and crackling and hissing. Then the embers exploded like firecrackers.

"Whew!" exclaimed the Bascomb father. "What in the world is in those logs?"

"Perhaps they are bewitched," said the Bascomb boy. "But Spooky is napping through it all," said the Bascomb girl. "And there's a grin on his face."

That night Spooky went through the little door in the big door. He went pussyfoot, pussyfoot to the bed of begonias. He lay there for a long time. No bats came to bother him, and after a time Snowball came outside to enjoy the sounds of the night.